# The Collapse:
# The Road to Sanctuary

Vanida Plamondon

THE COLLAPSE: THE ROAD TO SANCTUARY

**First edition. December 24, 2024.**



ISBN: 979-8230935988

Written by Vanida Plamondon.

Kane got me this journal so I can write down my story. I am writing these first handful of entries from memory.

When I opened my eyes, the first thing I noticed was the buzzing light above me. It flickered like it couldn't quite decide if it wanted to stay on or give up entirely. The room smelled like antiseptic and something else—something stale, like old cardboard left out in the rain. My head felt foggy, like I'd been swimming too deep and couldn't quite surface.

A nurse was leaning over me, her face lined with years that didn't seem entirely kind. Her name tag said "Marla," but it looked scratched, like someone had tried to rub the letters away. She didn't smile when she saw I was awake. "You're up," she said, not unkindly, but not warmly either. She checked the machines next to me, muttering numbers under her breath like they were secrets meant just for her.

I tried to sit up, but everything ached. My muscles felt like they'd forgotten their job. "Where am I?" My voice cracked, and it felt foreign, like it belonged to someone else.

"Renewal Horizons," Marla replied. "Non-profit hospital. Lucky you. Most folks wouldn't get this kind of care for free."

The name meant nothing to me. "How long was I out?" I asked. My head throbbed with every word, like someone was knocking on the inside of my skull.

"Long enough," she said. Her face softened a little, almost like she was deciding I deserved a bit of pity after all. "You were found in one of those old bunkers. Lucky someone dug you up. Most people don't make it out of those things alive."

Bunker? I couldn't make sense of it. I tried to piece together the last thing I remembered, but my brain felt like Swiss cheese. Holes everywhere, nothing solid to hold on to.

Marla handed me a stack of papers and a pen. "Discharge forms. Sign here, here, and here. We'll get you out of our hair soon enough." She said it like I was some stray cat they'd been feeding out of guilt.

As I scribbled my name—at least I remembered that much—a volunteer popped their head in. Young, maybe twenty, with wide eyes that looked like they hadn't seen enough sleep. "Hey," they said casually, "what year do you think it is?"

"2026," I answered without hesitation. The volunteer's face froze, like I'd just told them their pet had died. Then they laughed, a little too loud.

"Oh, honey," they said, "a lot's happened since then. You might wanna head to the nearest Women's Protective Asylum before it gets dark." They said it so breezily, like they were giving me directions to the nearest gas station.

Before I could ask what they meant, they were gone, leaving me with a sinking feeling in my gut and a head full of questions I wasn't sure I wanted the answers to.

# March 13, The Ambulance

I was still trying to make sense of what the volunteer had said when I heard it. A low rumble, like distant thunder, growing louder. The walls seemed to vibrate with it. Through the grimy window near my bed, I caught sight of something pulling up to the hospital entrance. At first, I thought it was a delivery truck, but then I saw the words painted in bold letters along the side: Austin Retrieval Services. The vehicle looked like an ambulance that had gone to war and come back with a few souvenirs. Steel plates covered the windows, and the whole thing was scratched up like it had been clawed by a giant.

Before I could process it, the back doors swung open, and two medics jumped out. Except, they weren't just medics. They wore tactical gear, helmets with tinted visors, and vests bristling with equipment. They looked like soldiers playing dress-up as paramedics. Between them, they hauled a man who was screaming and thrashing, though one leg dangled at an odd angle. His uniform was blue, but it was hard to tell with all the blood. A cop, I realized, though he looked more like a rag doll someone had been rough with.

I couldn't look away. The medics barked orders at each other, their movements quick and practised. They didn't seem bothered by the blood or the screams. One of them yanked open the emergency room door with a clang that echoed down the hall.

My stomach knotted. Something about the whole scene felt wrong, like I was watching a movie I wasn't supposed to see. I didn't wait to find out what happened next. My instincts kicked in, sharp and clear for the first time since I'd woken up. I pulled myself out of the bed, every muscle in my body protesting, and grabbed the clothes folded on the chair. They were stiff and smelled like they'd been washed in a sink.

I slipped into the hallway, keeping close to the wall. The place was eerily quiet, the kind of quiet that made every sound—my breathing, the shuffle of my bare feet—feel too loud. The exit sign glowed faintly at the far end, like it was offering a lifeline. I made my way toward it, past doors that were mostly shut but not always. One was ajar, revealing a room piled high with boxes and what looked like canned food. Another had a patient inside, lying so still I couldn't tell if they were breathing.

When I reached the stairwell, I hesitated. I glanced back toward the ER. I could hear the medics now, their boots pounding on the tile, their voices clipped and efficient. I didn't stick around to hear more. I pushed the door open and slipped into the stairwell, the heavy metal door shutting behind me with a dull thud.

I took the stairs two at a time, ignoring the pain in my legs. At the bottom, I paused, listening for any sign of movement. There was nothing but the faint hum of a vending machine. I pushed open the door to the lobby and stepped out into the night, the cool air hitting me like a slap.

I didn't know where I was going, but I knew I had to get far away from that hospital and whatever nightmare I'd just stumbled out of.

Venturing out into the street, I felt like I'd wandered into someone else's fever dream. The air had that heavy stillness, like the city itself was holding its breath. The buildings were still there, most of them at least, but they didn't look quite right. Some had barricades slapped across their entrances—sheets of metal, wooden planks, even the occasional stack of sandbags. A few windows glinted with the unmistakable flash of broken glass, while others were sealed tight with what looked like makeshift shutters.

The streets were almost empty, but not quite. A low rumble made me jump, and I ducked behind a parked car. A vehicle rolled past, slow and deliberate, its armour glinting under the pale light of a flickering streetlamp. It looked more like a tank than a car, with thick steel plating and a turret-like thing on the roof. The windows were dark, and I couldn't tell who—or what—was inside. It vanished around the corner, leaving me frozen in its wake.

I crept out from my hiding spot and started walking, keeping to the shadows. There were people too, moving in clusters like they were on some grim school field trip. Every single one of them was armed. Some carried rifles slung across their backs, others had pistols holstered at their sides. One guy had a machete strapped to his belt like he was expecting to hack through a jungle—or something worse. They walked with purpose, heads on swivels, eyes scanning the street like they were waiting for trouble to jump out and introduce itself.

Nobody looked at me. Maybe they didn't care, or maybe I just looked like part of the scenery in my faded hospital scrubs. Either way, I wasn't about to draw their attention. I kept moving, my footsteps as light as I could manage on the cracked pavement. The road was littered with debris—scraps of metal, shattered glass, and what looked suspiciously like the remnants of someone's backpack.

It wasn't the complete wasteland I'd imagined from movies. Some buildings had lights on, dim and flickering but still there. A convenience store had a glowing open sign in the window, though the bars across the door made it clear you couldn't just stroll in. A diner on the corner looked like it was in business, the neon sign buzzing faintly, though I wasn't about to test my luck by walking in. Everything felt like it was holding together by sheer stubbornness, as though the city refused to collapse completely, even if it was well on its way.

The farther I walked, the clearer it became that this wasn't just a bad neighbourhood or a rough night. Something big had gone wrong, and it had left its fingerprints on everything.

I tried keeping to the shadows, but eventually, I came face-to-face with a group of people. It happened near an old gas station, where I'd ducked behind a rusted-out truck to catch my breath. The group rounded the corner before I even heard them, their boots crunching on the gravel like they had somewhere important to be. There were five of them, all dressed like they'd raided a tactical gear warehouse. One had a shotgun resting casually on his shoulder, another carried a rifle strapped across his chest, and a woman in the middle gripped a machete that looked like it had seen plenty of action.

They spotted me before I could back away, and for a second, I thought I was done for. The woman with the machete tilted her head, sizing me up like I was some kind of curiosity. "You lost?" she asked, her voice sharp enough to cut glass.

I swallowed hard and nodded. "Yeah. Just trying to figure out what's going on."

The man with the shotgun snorted. "What's going on? You serious?" He looked at the others, like I'd just told a bad joke.

The machete woman stepped closer, her eyes narrowing. "You from one of the shelters?" she asked. Her tone wasn't friendly, but it wasn't outright hostile either. Suspicious, maybe, like she was waiting for me to slip up.

I shook my head, trying to keep my voice steady. "No. I just... woke up. In a hospital. They said—well, they didn't say much of anything, really."

That got their attention. They exchanged looks, and the guy with the rifle muttered something I couldn't catch. "You don't know?" the woman asked, her grip tightening on the machete. "About the collapse? About the zones?"

I shook my head again, feeling more like an idiot by the second. "I don't even know what year it is," I admitted, which was apparently the wrong thing to say. They all froze, their faces a mix of confusion and disbelief.

"What year do you think it is?" the shotgun guy asked, his tone more cautious now.

"2026," I said, and that did it. They looked at each other like I'd just sprouted another head.

"You're joking," the machete woman said, her voice low. "You have to be joking."

"I'm not," I said, holding up my hands. "I swear, I don't know what's going on. Please, just tell me what happened."

They didn't answer right away. They just stood there, watching me like I was some kind of puzzle they couldn't figure out. Finally, the machete woman shook her head. "You need to get off the street," she said. "Now. Before someone decides you're worth the trouble."

I opened my mouth to ask what she meant, but the shotgun guy cut me off. "She's not gonna last five minutes out here," he said. "Look at her."

"She's not our problem," the rifle guy shot back.

They started arguing, their voices low but heated, and I realized I wasn't going to get much more out of them. Whatever had happened to the world, it had left everyone on edge, and I wasn't about to push my luck. "Thanks for the advice," I said, edging away. "I'll figure it out."

The machete woman gave me a long, hard look, then nodded. "Good luck," she said, though it didn't sound like she meant it.

A few blocks later, I found myself standing in front of a battered community board. It was one of those corkboard things you see outside coffee shops, except this one looked like it had been through a war. The frame was cracked, and most of the flyers were torn or faded beyond recognition. One, though, caught my eye. It was bright orange and pinned up with what looked like a rusty nail. The bold black letters across the top read: "KNOW YOUR SENTINEL CORPSEC RIGHTS!"

I tugged it down and smoothed out the creases, scanning the text. It was a strange mix of propaganda and warning. "Sentinel CorpSec forces are authorized to operate in all zones for public safety," it read. Below that was a list of rules: cooperate with Sentinel CorpSec personnel, keep identification visible, curfews strictly enforced. The words sounded official, but something about them felt off. At the bottom, there was a note about corporate jurisdictions and zones, followed by a line that hit me like a punch to the gut: "In the wake of federal destabilization, Sentinel CorpSec ensures order in the absence of centralized governance."

I stared at the flyer, my fingers trembling. Federal destabilization? Sentinel CorpSec? I read it again, my brain struggling to connect the dots. What did they mean by "absence of centralized governance"? The government didn't just vanish, did it? I glanced around the empty street, the fortified buildings, the armoured vehicles. It all started to make a sick kind of sense.

My knees wobbled, and I leaned against a lamppost to steady myself. The question I'd been trying to push aside came roaring back. What year was it? The hospital volunteer, the group with the machete woman—they'd all reacted like I was insane for thinking it was 2026. But if it wasn't 2026, then when was it?

And what about my family? My friends? The life I'd left behind, wherever—or whenever—that was? I clutched the flyer like it could somehow give me answers, even though all it had done was pile on more questions.

Night had started to fall, and the streets grew eerily quiet. The armoured vehicles I'd seen earlier had thinned out, replaced by a suffocating stillness. I decided to duck down a narrow alley, hoping to avoid anyone who might ask too many questions. That's when I heard the hum. It was low and steady at first, like a generator in the distance. Then it got louder, sharper, and the unmistakable sound of boots on pavement followed.

I froze, pressing myself against a crumbling brick wall. A group of Sentinel CorpSec officers turned the corner, their armoured helmets gleaming under the flickering streetlights. There were four of them, all carrying weapons that looked more advanced than anything I'd ever seen, even in action movies.

One of them barked into a handheld radio, and another scanned the alley with a flashlight mounted on his rifle. I didn't need to hear the words to know what was happening. They were looking for someone, and judging by the curfew notice I'd seen earlier, it was probably anyone dumb enough to be out after dark. That someone was me.

The beam of light swept closer, and my heart pounded so hard I thought it might give me away. I crouched behind a dumpster, trying to make myself as small as possible. The officer with the flashlight stopped, his shadow falling long and dark across the alley. I could hear the faint crackle of his radio and the shuffle of his boots as he stepped closer.

Before he could reach me, a hand clamped over my mouth, pulling me backward into the darkness. I struggled for a second before realizing whoever it was wasn't wearing Sentinel CorpSec armour. The grip was strong but not rough. The stranger whispered, "Quiet," and I caught a glimpse of his face in the dim light. Sharp features, a buzz cut, and eyes that looked like they'd seen too much. He wore a plain black jacket and a utility belt loaded with gear.

I didn't have much choice but to trust him. He moved quickly, keeping me low as he led me farther into the shadows. The Sentinel CorpSec patrol didn't seem to notice, their flashlight sweeping past the spot where we'd just been. After what felt like an eternity, the hum of their vehicle faded into the distance.

The man let go of me and stood, brushing off his hands like saving people was just another part of his day. "You've got a death wish or what?" he said, his voice calm and flat.

I stared at him, still catching my breath. "Who are you?"

"Kane," he said, like that was all the explanation I needed. "You're lucky I found you first. CorpSec doesn't ask questions before they drag you off."

"Why did you help me?" I asked, my voice shakier than I wanted it to be.

He shrugged. "You looked like you needed it." He glanced at the flyer I was still clutching, then at me. "You're not from around here, are you?"

I shook my head, still trying to process everything. "I... I don't even know what's going on."

Kane gave me a long look, like he was sizing me up. "Yeah, I figured. Come on," he said, nodding toward the darkened street. "You'll last about five minutes out here on your own."

Kane didn't say much as we walked, his eyes constantly scanning the darkened streets. He moved with a quiet confidence, like he'd been doing this his whole life. I stumbled along behind him, clutching the edges of my hospital gown and feeling about as useful as a screen door on a submarine. Finally, when we reached a half-collapsed diner with its windows boarded up, he stopped and turned to face me.

"Alright," he said, his voice low but firm. "Here's the deal. I'm not in the charity business. If you want protection, you pay for it."

I blinked at him, my brain taking a moment to catch up. "Pay you? With what? I don't even have shoes."

Kane sighed, rubbing the bridge of his nose like I was the world's most frustrating puzzle. "Figures. Look, I don't work for free. People like me—" He stopped himself, his jaw tightening. "Forget it. Point is, this isn't a free ride."

"People like you?" I asked, ignoring the way he glared at me for prying. "What's that supposed to mean?"

He crossed his arms, his jacket shifting just enough for me to catch a glimpse of the pistol holstered at his side. "Used to be CorpSec," he admitted, his tone flat. "Now I work for myself. Security, escorts, retrievals—you name it. And it's not cheap."

The pieces clicked together in my head, but they didn't make me feel any safer. "So you're one of them," I said, a little sharper than I intended.

Kane's expression darkened, but he didn't take the bait. "Not anymore," he said simply. He studied me for a moment, his eyes narrowing. "You're really clueless, aren't you? You don't know where you are, who runs this place, or what'll happen if you keep wandering around like a lost puppy."

"I didn't ask to be here," I snapped. "I woke up in a hospital, and everyone acts like I should know what's going on. I don't even know what year it is."

That made him pause. For the first time, his guarded expression cracked just enough for me to see a flicker of something—pity, maybe, or curiosity. He let out a long breath, then muttered something under his breath that sounded like "damn it."

"Alright," he said grudgingly. "No money, no plan, no clue. Fine. I'll get you out of the city. But don't expect me to hold your hand."

"Why are you helping me?" I asked, suspicious.

Kane shrugged, already turning toward the diner. "Because if I don't, someone else will find you. And trust me, they won't be as nice about it."

I wasn't sure if I believed him, but I didn't exactly have better options. Kane pushed open a side door to the diner, motioning for me to follow. "Get inside. We'll figure out the rest in the morning."

Reluctantly, I stepped into the shadows, wondering just how far I could trust someone who used to work for the same people hunting me down.

We found Quinn rummaging through what was left of a corner store, her wiry frame half-buried in the wreckage of overturned shelves and broken glass. She moved fast, her fingers darting through the debris like a pianist searching for the right keys. Kane stopped in the doorway, his hand resting lightly on the pistol at his hip.

"Quinn," he said, his voice carrying just enough edge to make her flinch. She looked up, a smirk spreading across her dirt-smudged face when she saw him.

"Well, if it isn't the great Kane," she said, brushing her hands off on her patched cargo pants. "Still playing babysitter, I see."

I bristled at the remark, but Kane didn't take the bait. "We're looking for supplies," he said. "Got anything useful?"

Quinn leaned back against the counter, crossing her arms. "Define 'useful.' And what's in it for me?"

Kane's jaw tightened, but I spoke up before he could. "You're scavenging in a city that looks like it's been through a war. Maybe you could help someone for once instead of just thinking about yourself."

Quinn raised an eyebrow, her smirk widening. "Feisty. I like her. What's your name, new girl?"

"Ariel," I said, feeling the urge to match her energy. "And you are?"

"Quinn," she said with a mock bow. "Master of finding things people didn't know they needed. Or wanted. Or left behind. And, on occasion, professional coward."

"That last bit's true enough," Kane muttered, stepping past me to inspect her haul. "But she's got her uses."

Quinn rolled her eyes but didn't argue. "Don't listen to him. I'm just strategic. Why fight when you can sneak, grab what you need, and get out before anyone notices?"

"That's a nice way of saying you leave people behind when things go south," Kane said, sorting through a pile of canned goods she'd stacked on the counter.

Quinn shrugged, unbothered. "Better me than both of us, right?"

I wasn't sure how to feel about her yet. She seemed clever and quick, but there was a glint in her eye that made me wonder if Kane was right to keep her at arm's length. Still, she didn't seem like a threat, at least not to me.

"So," Quinn said, pulling out a dented can of peaches and tossing it in my direction. I fumbled but caught it. "You're lost, confused, and tagging along with Mr. Sunshine over there. What's your story?"

I hesitated, not sure how much to share. "I... just woke up," I said finally. "In a hospital. Everything's different. I don't even know how it got like this."

Quinn whistled low, leaning on the counter. "Fresh out of the time capsule, huh? That explains the deer-in-headlights look. Don't worry, stick with me and you'll catch on quick."

Kane snorted, grabbing a backpack from the floor. "We're not sticking with you. We're moving out as soon as we've got what we need."

Quinn pouted theatrically. "Oh, come on, Kane. You know you'll need someone who can get you into places. And out, if it comes to that."

Kane didn't answer, but I caught the flicker of consideration in his eyes. Something told me that, whether he liked it or not, Quinn wasn't going anywhere.

We sat around a fire Quinn had coaxed to life in an old trash barrel, the flickering flames casting shadows on the cracked walls of the abandoned gas station we'd holed up in. Kane leaned against the far wall, cleaning his gun with the practised ease of someone who didn't trust a moment of quiet. Quinn perched on an overturned crate, tossing a small knife from hand to hand as she talked.

"So, here's the gist, new girl," she said, her voice light but with an edge that suggested she wasn't spinning a bedtime story. "After Trump's little tantrum back in '27 and that mess of a coup, everything started falling apart. The government couldn't hold it together, and the corporations stepped in, all noble-like, saying they'd keep things running. Except, surprise, they only kept things running for themselves."

Kane looked up, his expression as blank as ever. "Corporations divided up the country like a pie. Each one took a slice. They call them regions now, but it's just territories where they make the rules. No federal oversight, no elections, just Sentinel CorpSec enforcing their bottom line."

Quinn let out a short laugh. "Yeah, and by enforcing, he means cracking skulls and dragging people off if they can't pay their dues. Most of us are just trying to survive. That's why the streets look like they do. No one trusts anyone, and everyone's out for themselves."

I hugged my knees, trying to process what they were saying. It felt like a nightmare I couldn't wake up from. "But... what about the military? Or the police?"

"Some stayed loyal," Kane said, his voice flat. "Most didn't. Now you've got mercenary groups, private security forces, and whatever's left of local law enforcement scrambling to keep their own corners in check. It's chaos."

Quinn leaned forward, her smirk softening into something close to sympathy. "Canada's different, though. They didn't let the corps take over. They've got rules, real ones. People there still have rights. That's where you want to be."

"That's where I need to be," I said quietly, more to myself than to them.

Kane nodded, his eyes narrowing. "It's not going to be easy. The highways are dangerous, and CorpSec doesn't like anyone crossing borders without permission."

Quinn twirled her knife, the blade catching the firelight. "But it's doable. And honestly? I wouldn't mind getting out of this dumpster fire of a country myself."

"You'd come with us?" I asked, surprised.

She shrugged, a grin tugging at her lips. "You seem nice enough, and you clearly need someone who knows how to get around without getting shot. Plus, Canada sounds like a good place to start over."

Kane didn't argue, which I took as a sign he'd already decided having Quinn along wasn't the worst idea. I wasn't sure how I'd landed in this strange trio, but for the first time since waking up, I felt like I might have a chance. Even if it was slim, it was a chance.

Kane led the way down a dark alley, his steps quick but steady, like he knew exactly where we were headed. Quinn stayed close, her eyes darting around as if she expected someone to jump out of the shadows at any moment. I tried to keep up, still feeling like a fish out of water, but I followed them, trusting their lead.

"We're going to need more than just what we can scrounge from here," Kane said over his shoulder. "I've got a contact who can get us what we need, but she's... not exactly the easiest person to work with."

Quinn chuckled. "You mean Zara, right? The 'cop' who's more about looking good in her uniform than actually doing any real policing?"

Kane grunted in agreement. "That's her. She'll help, though. If the price is right."

When we reached her place, it wasn't what I expected. I thought maybe we'd find her in some rundown precinct or a fortified office building, but no. It was a high-rise apartment with polished floors and a view of the city, though the windows were mostly covered by thick, white curtains that blocked out any sign of the chaos outside. Zara was perched on a leather sofa, flipping through a fashion magazine, her perfectly manicured nails tapping on the pages.

"Hey, Kane," she said without looking up. "And who's this?" Her tone wasn't unfriendly, but it was cold and calculating, like she was sizing me up before I even said a word.

"This is Ariel," Kane said, nodding at me. "We need gear. Serious stuff. And we need to get to Canada."

Zara finally looked up, her eyes narrowing slightly as she studied me. "Canada? That's ambitious. You know it's not like it used to be, right? Borders are locked down tight."

"Yeah, we know," I said, trying to sound like I wasn't completely out of my depth. "But we need to get there, no matter what."

Zara shrugged, her expression shifting to one of mild disinterest. "Sounds like a headache. What do I get out of it?"

Kane gave her a hard look. "You get paid. You help us, we make it worth your while. You know how this works."

She smirked, flipping another page in her magazine. "Yeah, I know. But I've got a reputation to maintain, so I'll need something more than just cash. You want me to put myself at risk for you? You better make it worth my time, Kane."

I was starting to get a picture of what kind of person Zara was. She wasn't about doing the right thing or helping people. She was about power, status, and the perks that came with it. But in a place like this, I figured she was probably one of the few people who could actually get us what we needed.

"What do you want?" I asked, surprised by my own boldness.

Zara smiled, a slow, calculating smile that didn't quite reach her eyes. "Well, since you're asking, I think you'll find I like to have things on my terms. And right now, my terms are simple: I'll help you, but I expect you to keep a little distance from me when we're out there. I don't need people thinking I'm slumming it with the likes of you."

Kane sighed, but nodded. "Fine. We'll stick to the plan, just get us what we need."

Zara stood up, tossing the magazine aside like it was no longer worth her time. "I'll have the gear ready by tomorrow. Be here, bright and early. Don't be late."

As we turned to leave, Quinn muttered under her breath, "She's a piece of work, isn't she?"

I nodded, still trying to shake the feeling that this whole plan was starting to feel more like a game than a life-or-death mission. But I had no choice. I needed to get to Canada, and Zara was our ticket.

The sun was just starting to dip below the horizon as we set out, the cityscape of Austin stretching out in front of us, its broken streets and derelict buildings a harsh reminder of the world we'd found ourselves in. Kane was in front, his steps heavy but purposeful, like he'd been walking these streets for years. Quinn trailed behind us, always a few paces back, glancing over her shoulder every now and then as if expecting someone to follow.

I couldn't shake the feeling that this whole thing, this entire journey, was bigger than just getting to Canada. It felt like we were headed toward some kind of reckoning, whether we were ready for it or not.

Kane wasn't much of a talker, but as we moved through the ruins, I noticed something in the way he carried himself—like he was constantly on edge, like there was a storm brewing inside him. Every so often, I caught his eyes lingering on something distant, some dark memory I wasn't sure I wanted to know about.

"Been a long time since I've had to watch out for someone," Kane muttered as we stopped for a quick rest near an abandoned building. His voice was low, almost guarded, but there was a kind of weariness to it that made me want to press further.

I sat down beside him, trying to keep the conversation light. "What's that supposed to mean?"

He let out a breath, glancing down at his hands, almost like he was inspecting them for some kind of unseen stain. "I used to be in Sentinel CorpSec," he said quietly, not meeting my eyes. "Did things... things I'm not proud of."

I didn't say anything at first. I could feel the weight of his words hanging between us, thick and heavy. There was a part of me that wanted to ask what exactly he'd done, to push him to share it all, but I didn't. Instead, I just nodded, letting him take the lead.

"I was good at it," he continued, his voice almost detached now, as if he was talking about someone else entirely. "Good at breaking people down, making them disappear... whatever it took to keep the order. I didn't care who got hurt, as long as I got paid."

I felt a pang in my chest, like I could almost feel the regret in his voice. "But you don't do that anymore, right?" I asked softly, glancing up at him.

His laugh was dark, almost bitter. "You think I'd still be here if I did?" Kane shook his head. "I was good at what I did, but I couldn't keep doing it. I lost something along the way. I don't know what it is, but it's gone now."

I thought about his words for a moment, letting the silence stretch between us. It was a strange thing to hear from someone who had been so calm, so methodical, so ready to take on anything. I hadn't expected him to open up like that, especially not to me.

"You're not the same person you were," I said quietly. "You're here. You're helping. That's got to mean something."

Kane looked at me then, really looked at me, like he was trying to figure me out. "I don't know if it does," he muttered, his voice low. "I don't know if I'm even capable of being that person anymore. Maybe it's just too late for me to change."

I could see the struggle in his eyes. It wasn't just physical exhaustion—it was something deeper, something he hadn't let anyone see until now. I didn't know if I could fix him or even if that was my job, but I felt this surge of something I couldn't quite explain. Compassion? Hope? It was the kind of thing that kept me going, even when everything seemed pointless.

"You're not beyond it, Kane," I said gently. "Maybe you think you are, but you're not. People can change, even when they don't believe they can."

He looked at me again, his gaze sharp, but something softened there, just for a moment. "Maybe you're right," he said, the words barely a whisper, like he was tasting them for the first time. "I don't know. But... thanks, I guess."

I didn't say anything more. There was no need to. I knew he wasn't ready to believe it fully. He still had a long way to go, and maybe I didn't have all the answers. But I did know one thing for sure—if there was any chance of him finding some part of himself again, it would take more than just the promise of survival. It would take kindness, and maybe, just maybe, a little bit of hope.

We stayed like that for a few moments, the night settling in around us, the distant hum of the city a constant reminder of how far we were from where we used to be. Kane's armour seemed a little heavier tonight, but I could tell it wasn't just the weight of the gear. It was the weight of his past, pressing down on him, and I wasn't sure if he'd ever be able to shake it off.

But maybe, just maybe, he'd start to believe that he could.

We were moving through the outskirts of Austin, the cracked streets and rubble all too familiar now, when we spotted them. A family, huddled together under the overhang of a partially collapsed building. The mother, her clothes torn and dusty, was holding a small child close to her chest, while a man, maybe her husband, stood protectively by her side, his eyes scanning the street nervously.

Kane stopped, his usual stoic expression shifting for a second as he sized up the situation. Quinn, always quick to assess, muttered something about checking their gear, but it was obvious we weren't going to just leave them there. The family was obviously struggling, and in a world like this, that meant they were vulnerable.

"Do we help?" Quinn asked, though I could tell by the look in her eyes she wasn't too keen on getting involved.

Kane glanced at her, then back at the family. There was a moment of hesitation, just a flicker of doubt in his usually hard gaze. I could see the conflict brewing inside him. He wasn't the type to go out of his way for anyone, least of all strangers in this broken world. But when his eyes met mine, something shifted, and the decision was made.

"Yeah," Kane said, his voice gruff, "We help."

I wasn't sure what surprised me more—the fact that Kane had agreed or the way the family's faces seemed to soften at his words. It wasn't much, but to them, it was everything.

As we approached, the man straightened up, trying to look tougher than he probably felt. The woman, who hadn't looked up until then, finally made eye contact with me. Her eyes were full of fear, but there was something else there too—a kind of quiet strength, like she was fighting to keep it together for the sake of her child.

Kane wasted no time. "What happened?" he asked, his tone blunt but not unkind.

The man, who introduced himself as Marcus, gave a quick glance at his wife before speaking. "We've been trying to get to Canada. The roads are bad, and our supplies are running low. But it's the women—" He stopped, his jaw tightening. "It's the women who are suffering the most. Forced into these... these places. Asylums. Labour camps. You've heard of them, right?"

I nodded, though I didn't know what to say. The way Marcus spoke made it clear this wasn't just a personal crisis—it was part of a much bigger problem. The woman, who had remained silent until now, finally spoke up, her voice shaking but determined.

"They call it 'protecting societal order,'" she said, her words laced with bitterness. "They don't care about our lives. They only care about control. Women—especially women with children—are treated like property now. If we're not sent to an asylum, we're forced into labour camps. Work to 'restore order.' It's not about survival. It's about keeping us in line."

Her voice cracked at the end, and I could feel the weight of her words. It was one thing to hear about it secondhand, but to hear it from someone living through it, someone who had experienced it firsthand—it hit harder than I expected.

"I'm sorry," I whispered, not knowing what else to say. I wasn't sure if my sympathy helped or if it was just a hollow comfort in a world that had lost its sense of compassion.

Kane, usually the one who didn't flinch in the face of hardship, shifted uncomfortably. I could tell that what the woman had said struck a nerve. He turned his attention back to Marcus. "You know how to get to Canada?" he asked, his tone steady, though I could tell it was more of a challenge than a question.

"We've heard there's a safe route up through the mountains," Marcus replied. "But we can't go alone. We've got nowhere to go if we don't find help."

There was a pause, a long stretch of silence where the decision hung in the air. I could feel the weight of it pressing down on us, but I knew Kane wasn't the kind of guy to make promises lightly. Still, he didn't hesitate.

"We'll take you as far as we can," he said, his voice rough. "But you need to understand—this is dangerous. The roads aren't safe, and we'll need to move quickly."

The relief on the woman's face was immediate, though it was mixed with a touch of uncertainty. She glanced down at her child, then back at us. "Thank you," she whispered, the words carrying more gratitude than she probably intended.

As we began to move out, I noticed something in Kane's posture that wasn't there before—a slight softening in his shoulders, like a burden had been lifted. I wasn't sure if it was because he knew the family was now under his protection, or if it was something more. Something in him was changing, and though he probably wouldn't admit it, I could see the seeds of it being planted.

We walked in silence for a while, the quiet of the streets broken only by our footsteps and the occasional distant sound of gunfire or shouting. But even amidst the chaos, I could feel a shift in the air. Kane wasn't the same person he had been when I first met him. And as much as he might deny it, I knew something inside him was waking up, just like I was waking up to this new, broken world around us.

The further we walked, the more the weight of the world seemed to press down on us. But for the first time, it didn't feel so hopeless. Not with Kane, Quinn, and even the family we had just met. We were all in this together, even if the world had tried to break us apart.

We had been travelling for a few days, the sun dipping lower in the sky, casting long shadows across the ruined landscape. The group was quieter now, more alert, and the weight of the journey seemed to settle on all of us. The road was still deserted, save for the occasional rustle of wind or distant creak of metal from a building swaying precariously in the breeze. We moved in a tight formation, the family now trailing behind Kane and Quinn, with me taking up the rear, keeping a watchful eye on our surroundings.

The silence was almost oppressive. No one spoke much anymore, but I could feel the tension in the air. It wasn't just the atmosphere of the ruined world around us; it was something more. Something was off.

I caught a glimpse of Quinn looking over her shoulder, her eyes darting nervously. She muttered something about a bad feeling, but Kane was the one to react first.

"We're not alone," he muttered under his breath, his hand drifting to the hilt of his weapon.

I felt a jolt of fear in my chest. My eyes scanned the deserted road, trying to make sense of it. At first, I didn't see anything, but then I noticed movement—just a flicker at the edge of my vision.

"Get down," Kane snapped.

Before I could even react, I felt myself shoved roughly to the ground, my heart pounding in my ears. I looked up to see Kane and Quinn already crouched low, their eyes scanning the surroundings with practised precision. The family, confused and terrified, followed suit, huddling together as best they could.

And then it happened—like a storm breaking. Figures emerged from the shadows, like predators stalking their prey. At first, it was just one, then two, then a whole gang of them. Dirty, dishevelled, and armed with everything from knives to rusty rifles, they moved with alarming speed. Their faces were covered in dirt and grime, their eyes wild with a mix of desperation and malice.

"Look what we've got here," one of them called out, his voice high-pitched and mocking. "A nice little group of travellers. Must be worth something, right?"

Kane didn't flinch. His hand remained steady, gripping his gun with a firm resolve. "Stay behind me," he said to the family, his voice low and controlled.

The gang leader—if you could call him that—stepped forward, grinning like a wolf ready to pounce. "Now, we don't want any trouble," he said, his voice dripping with sarcasm. "Just hand over what you've got. Weapons, food, water. All of it."

I could feel the panic rising in my chest, but I kept my mouth shut. I wasn't sure what to do in this situation. We were outnumbered, and the gang clearly had no intentions of negotiating.

Quinn, surprisingly, spoke up. "You really want to do this?" she called, her voice laced with nervous bravado.

The gang members laughed, a few of them taking a few steps closer, their weapons raised. "Oh, we're doing this," the leader said, his grin widening.

Kane was already moving, silent and fast. In one smooth motion, he aimed his weapon and fired. The shot rang out, echoing down the empty road, and one of the attackers went down with a sharp cry. It wasn't a fatal shot, but it was enough to make them hesitate.

"Run!" Kane shouted, and without waiting for anyone to respond, he was already on the move, leading the way.

Quinn followed quickly, pulling the family along with her. I didn't need any encouragement. I pushed myself to my feet, nearly tripping over my own legs, and sprinted after them. The sound of pounding footsteps and shouts echoed behind us, but I dared not look back.

We didn't make it far. The gang was relentless, staying close enough to keep up but not close enough to catch us—yet. As we turned a corner, we were cut off by another group of marauders, this time from the other side. We were surrounded.

I could feel the cold sweat forming on the back of my neck, my breath coming in ragged gasps. Kane's face was hard, his eyes calculating. He wasn't panicking, but I could tell this wasn't a fight we could win.

"This is it," I whispered to myself, though I couldn't tell if I was trying to convince myself or not.

Kane didn't seem ready to give up. He moved quickly, pulling a grenade from his vest and tossing it behind him. The explosion wasn't huge, but it was enough to send several of the gang members scrambling. For a split second, we had a chance.

"Go! Now!" Kane barked.

We didn't need to be told twice. We bolted, running as fast as our legs would carry us. The family was close behind us, but I could hear the gang regrouping, closing in.

Then, out of nowhere, Quinn did something I never expected. She darted back toward the gang, pulling a few grenades from her pack and tossing them in their direction. It was a risky move, but it worked. The gang hesitated, their attention shifting as the grenades exploded, and we used the chaos to put more distance between us.

We didn't stop running until we were deep in the ruins of an old building, where Kane finally slowed us down. "We're not safe yet," he muttered, his breath coming hard. But there was a flicker of something in his eyes—a realization that we had survived. For now, at least.

But I knew it wasn't over. We'd barely escaped with our lives, and the road ahead was even more dangerous than before. The world was broken, and we were just trying to stay ahead of it. And as much as I wanted to believe things would get better, I wasn't sure we'd make it out alive. Not in this world. Not with the enemies we were facing.

But for the moment, we were alive. And that was something, at least.

We had been on the road for many more days, the weight of our situation pressing down on us like an unseen force. The air felt thick with the dust of a world crumbling under its own weight, and each day was a gamble. We moved cautiously, always looking over our shoulders, never knowing when another gang might pop up or CorpSec would decide to make an example out of us. Kane, Quinn, and I had become a well-oiled machine, working together without much need for words. But then there was Zara.

We had managed to secure a temporary hideout in an old, fortified warehouse—rusted metal walls and broken windows giving us just enough cover to catch our breath. Zara had been with us for a little while now, ever since Kane and Quinn had managed to talk her into joining the cause. To say she wasn't the easiest to work with would be an understatement. But we needed someone with her knowledge of the city and its routes, so we tolerated her vanity, her constant primping, and her obsession with her social standing.

It became clear quickly that Zara's idea of survival didn't quite line up with ours. While Kane and Quinn were busy checking our gear and making sure we had enough supplies to keep moving, Zara was... well, preoccupied. She had spent the better part of the last hour rearranging her few meagre possessions, all the while lamenting the state of her once-pristine uniforms. She didn't care about the weapons or the rations, not really. No, Zara cared about her appearance. She wanted to look the part, to hold onto whatever scraps of her former life she could.

And that was where things started to go wrong.

We had been talking strategy when I heard the first faint sound of footsteps—slow, deliberate, the unmistakable shuffle of boots across rubble. My heart skipped a beat. Quinn tensed, eyes narrowing as she scanned the surrounding area. But Zara didn't notice. She was too busy fidgeting with the straps of her bulletproof vest, trying to adjust it just so, as if the way it fit would make a difference in this new world.

"Zara," I hissed under my breath, my hand flying to her arm. "We have company. Get moving."

Her eyes barely registered the urgency in my voice as she sighed, flicking a strand of her hair out of her face with exaggerated grace. "Oh, please," she scoffed, her voice dripping with annoyance. "There's no need to panic. We have time."

Before I could respond, the sound of boots grew louder, and Kane's voice snapped into action. "Move! Now!" he ordered, his eyes flashing with a cold fury. But it was too late. Zara hadn't moved, not fast enough.

I saw the first of the armed figures rounding the corner of the building, the glint of steel in the fading light. They weren't alone.

"Zara!" Kane shouted, his voice now sharp with panic.

She finally looked up, her eyes wide, as she realized the danger we were in. But instead of running, she darted back toward the stack of crates where her precious belongings were stashed. "I need my—" she began, but the words died on her lips when the first gunshot rang out. The crack of it seemed to echo for miles, and for a moment, everything froze.

Zara didn't get her things. Instead, she ducked behind the crates just as the attackers opened fire. I could see her, crouched low, her face pale with fear, her arms wrapped protectively around her stuff.

But it was too late. Kane was already in motion, pulling me toward the exit, while Quinn was already picking off one of the attackers with a clean shot. The group was scrambling to get to cover, but Zara wasn't with us. She was still by those crates, still trying to grab whatever she thought would be the key to survival.

"Zara!" Kane shouted again, his voice urgent, but there was a tension in it now, a growl of anger. She had put all of us at risk.

I couldn't understand it. This was no longer the world where looking good mattered. We were fighting for survival. But Zara was too wrapped up in herself to see it. As the enemy closed in, I saw Kane hesitate. He glanced back at the crates, his jaw tight with anger and frustration. I could see the conflict in him, the need to protect, the responsibility he felt for the group. But saving Zara meant risking all of us.

The next few seconds felt like an eternity. I looked at Kane, then at Quinn, who was already moving forward, her gun trained on the approaching figures. "Go," I whispered, my voice barely audible over the gunfire.

Kane didn't hesitate. He pushed me forward, and we bolted.

Zara, at the last moment, realized her mistake. As we sprinted for cover, I saw her face twist with something like regret. But by then, it was too late. The attackers were closing in, and she had wasted precious time on something as meaningless as her vanity.

Kane, ever the professional, didn't stop. He couldn't afford to. We had to get out of there.

We regrouped as best we could, managing to find a safer route out of the warehouse, but Zara's mistake had cost us. She had nearly led to our destruction, all for the sake of holding on to something that no longer mattered.

She didn't speak much after that. Perhaps, deep down, she understood. Or maybe she was too embarrassed. Either way, she kept to herself, and the group grew quieter as we continued on our journey. The lesson had been learned the hard way: in this world, there was no room for vanity. Not when survival was the only thing that mattered.

We had been on the move, the miles stretching out behind us like a trail of forgotten promises. The road was never kind, and the world around us felt as if it were slowly crumbling into dust. But there was a glimmer of hope when we stumbled upon the commune—a self-sufficient place tucked away in the remnants of what had once been a thriving neighbourhood. The walls were patched together with salvaged materials, but there was something about the place that felt... calm. Peaceful, even. The people were friendly, if a little cautious, and the food smelled fresh, a rarity these days. For the first time in what felt like forever, I let myself believe we might actually catch a break.

We were led inside by a young woman named Isla, who gave us a quick tour of their modest compound. It wasn't much—just a handful of homes, a small garden, and a few supply caches. But it was safe. And for a moment, it felt like we had found something resembling normal.

Zara, of course, was all smiles. She had spent the last few days grumbling about how unkempt her uniform was, but the moment we crossed into the commune, she straightened up. Her vanity never seemed to take a break. Still, she was grateful for the chance to catch her breath.

At least, that's what I thought at first. But things began to shift when we met the leaders—an older couple named Walter and Agnes. They were kind enough, if a little wary, but I could see their eyes flicking over us with the sort of suspicion that only comes from living in a world gone to hell. After a quick meal, we were invited to sit with them in their communal hall. It was a large, open space with mismatched chairs and tables, all arranged around a fire pit in the centre. There was a warmth to the room, both literally and figuratively, but I knew better than to let my guard down completely.

Walter wasted no time getting to the point.

"We've got enough food and water to survive for a while," he said, his voice gravelly but not unfriendly. "But we've learned the hard way that we can't be too trusting. Resources are precious now. We've seen what happens when people get desperate."

Agnes, who had been standing quietly by the window, turned to look at us. "We can offer you supplies," she said, her voice soft but firm. "But there's a price."

Zara perked up at this. I could see her eyes glinting, as if she thought she was about to get something special. I, on the other hand, felt a knot form in my stomach. Kane's expression was unreadable, but I knew he was already thinking about how we'd get out of here if things went south. Quinn, ever the opportunist, was sizing up the room, already looking for an exit strategy.

Walter leaned in slightly, his gaze locking onto Zara. "We've got eyes on the streets. We know who you are. Your badge—" He nodded toward Zara's Sentinel CorpSec insignia. "—it's valuable. To us. And to others."

Zara's face tightened, and for a moment, I could see the struggle in her eyes. Her badge was her identity now. She'd worn it proudly when we met her, like it was some kind of shield. But now, that badge was worth more than we'd ever imagined.

"You want me to give it up?" Zara asked, her voice a little too sharp for comfort.

Walter didn't flinch. "If you want supplies to keep you going, yes. That badge will get us protection, maybe a little more security. It's a trade. You want to survive? Then you'll have to make sacrifices. We can't trust anyone who hasn't proven themselves."

Kane's hand twitched at his side, and I could see him weighing the situation in his mind. He had no love for CorpSec, but this wasn't about the badge. It was about the group. And Zara was the one holding us up.

Zara's eyes flickered between Walter and the rest of us, and I could almost hear the gears turning in her head. She had always been someone who valued appearances, who held onto the illusion of power like a lifeline. Giving up that badge would mean admitting something she wasn't ready to admit—not just to us, but to herself.

"This is ridiculous," she finally muttered, standing up from the table. "I've been with you all this time, and now you want to strip me of the only thing that matters?"

Kane's voice was steady, cutting through the tension. "Zara, they're just trying to protect their people. We don't have a choice."

Quinn, ever the pragmatist, leaned forward. "You want to keep playing at being CorpSec? Fine. But we're not going to get anywhere if you don't let go of that badge. If we're going to get to Canada, we need to work together."

For a moment, the room was silent, save for the crackling of the fire. I could see Zara's resolve begin to crack. She wanted to argue, to hold onto that sense of power, but the reality of the situation was sinking in. She wasn't just protecting herself anymore—she was protecting all of us. And if she didn't let go of that badge, we might not make it out of here at all.

Finally, with a sigh that seemed to carry all the weight of her frustration, Zara reached into her bag and pulled out the Sentinel CorpSec badge. She held it out toward Walter, her fingers trembling slightly.

"Fine," she said quietly. "Take it. But don't think this means I'm trusting you."

Walter nodded, taking the badge from her hand. "Thank you," he said simply, his expression softening just a fraction. "We'll make sure you get what you need."

As we stood to leave, I could see Zara's eyes lingering on the badge in Walter's hand, her face a mixture of anger and loss. But I also saw something else there—a quiet understanding. The world had changed, and she was starting to realize that holding on to the past wasn't going to save her. Not anymore.

As we prepared to leave, the members of the commune, particularly Walter and Agnes, began to speak more kindly to Zara. They saw something in her they could use. The skills she had once used to enforce the laws of a broken system could now be turned to protecting them in their little corner of the world. I could see it in their eyes—the hope that a former Sentinel CorpSec officer could bring some measure of security in this wild, lawless new world. They offered her a place to stay, a room in their small compound, and more than that, a role. They wanted her expertise, her knowledge of how things used to work, and maybe even how to defend against the worst the streets could throw at them. For a moment, Zara looked tempted, like maybe she could take them up on it, bury the past and make a new life here.

But then Quinn, ever the pragmatist, stepped in. She had a look in her eye that I'd seen before—calculating and cold, as if she was already planning how to cut and run. "We don't need her," she muttered, eyes narrowing as she looked at Zara. "She's just a liability. This place is too exposed. We can't afford to play nice with everyone."

Her voice was sharp, but there was a tremor underneath it, like she was trying to convince herself as much as the rest of us. It wasn't the first time I'd seen Quinn shrink from conflict or responsibility, and I could feel the pull to leave Zara behind, to cut ties and make the journey a little easier. But something in me bristled at that. The world had already stripped so many of us of our humanity; the least we could do was offer each other the kind of support that mattered.

I stepped forward, trying to keep my voice even and calm. "Quinn, we can't leave her behind. That's not who we are, not anymore. We're a team, and we don't just drop people when things get tough."

Zara, still quiet, looked at me like I was speaking a foreign language. She had her walls up, as usual, but there was something vulnerable in the way her eyes flickered when I spoke. It wasn't just about her—this was about survival, about remembering what made us human in a world that had forgotten.

Kane, for his part, was silent. I wasn't sure what he was thinking, but I knew he agreed with me. He always did, even if he never said much. His cold pragmatism had its limits. He wasn't a monster.

After a long silence, Zara spoke, her voice a little softer than it had been before. "I'm not staying here," she said, her tone steady, but there was a hint of something else there—something close to regret. "You don't know what it's like to be a CorpSec officer now. My precinct is gone. Overrun. Sentinel CorpSec's taken control. They've killed or... assimilated anyone who doesn't fall in line."

Her eyes dropped to the ground, and for the first time, I saw the weight of her words land in the air between us. She wasn't just running away from the collapse of her own life—she was running from the very organization she had once served, the organization that had left her out in the cold.

"I'm not safe here," Zara continued, her voice low but resolute. "They'll come for me. They'll come for all of you if I stay. They don't care about who we were—they care about control. And that means anyone who used to be on the inside is a threat to them. I have to go to Canada. It's the only place left where I can... be safe."

There was an edge of finality in her voice, and I knew then that there was no turning back for Zara. This was more than just a desire to find refuge—it was her only chance at survival. Her badge meant nothing now. To Sentinel CorpSec, she was expendable. To the commune, she was a potential tool, a weapon to be used for their own protection. But to her, this was a life-or-death decision.

Quinn, still restless, shook her head. "This is a mess," she muttered, but even she knew that Zara had a point. We couldn't leave her behind, not if we were going to keep moving forward. Even if it meant taking a risk.

I looked at Zara, and in that moment, I made a decision. "You're coming with us," I said firmly. "No one gets left behind. Not now."

Zara met my gaze, and for the first time since I'd known her, I saw a flicker of something like gratitude in her eyes. It wasn't much, but it was enough. She nodded, and for the first time, I felt like we were all on the same side. The road ahead was still uncertain, but at least we wouldn't be facing it alone. Not anymore.

The decision to let the family stay at the commune felt right, and as they made their way into the compound, I couldn't help but feel a sense of relief for them. They had been so desperate, so lost, that I couldn't imagine what it would have been like to turn them away. I think, deep down, everyone in the group felt that way. Kane, who rarely showed any signs of softness, gave the father a nod before they disappeared into the crowd, and Quinn, though she'd never openly admit it, seemed to be relieved too.

As we left the commune, it was quiet between us, the weight of what had just happened hanging in the air. We were all still processing it in our own ways, but I could feel the bond growing stronger, almost unspoken but there all the same. We had done something right for once, something that didn't involve running, fighting, or looking out only for ourselves. It felt strange, like we'd just stepped into a new chapter that we weren't entirely sure how to navigate.

But with every step we took away from that place, I felt the cracks showing—those same vulnerabilities that made the journey ahead feel even more daunting. Zara wasn't saying much, her mind clearly on the long road ahead, but I could tell she was still struggling with what had just happened. She didn't belong in the world she had once known, and even though she'd made a choice to leave it behind, it wasn't an easy one. And Kane, who had stepped into the role of leader, was wearing his doubts on his sleeve, despite his tough exterior. His eyes kept darting back to the road ahead, like he was expecting something—anything—to happen, and it probably would.

Quinn, as usual, couldn't sit still. Her mind was already racing, thinking about what supplies we'd need, where we'd go next. She was practical, but in the way of someone who feared being caught unprepared more than anything else. Her mind had already moved past the commune, but I could see her uncertainty in the way she kept glancing at the others. She might have made the call to leave Zara behind, but now she was clinging to this new, uncertain bond that had started to form between us.

I wasn't immune to it either. Despite all the progress, the weight of what we were doing hadn't fully hit me until now. The world we had once known—the one where families didn't have to fear every knock on the door, where laws weren't just words printed on paper, where people were more than commodities—was gone. The scars were everywhere, and they weren't just in the buildings or the roads. They were in us too. The longer we travelled, the more I realized how deeply those scars had rooted themselves into our hearts. We had all lost something, and maybe that's what kept us going: the hope that we could find something better, something worth fighting for.

As we walked toward the distant horizon, where the next leg of our journey awaited, it was hard not to feel the weight of that responsibility. The group felt stronger, no doubt, but we were still fragile. The world we were heading into wasn't just dangerous—it was unforgiving. There would be no easy way forward, but we had each other. And that, for better or worse, had to be enough.

The day had started like any other, the weight of the journey pressing down on us as we made our way through the cracked, forgotten highways that seemed to stretch on forever. But then came the telltale sign: the distant rumble of engines, the whirring of tires on gravel, and that sickening feeling that we were being watched. Kane, who had been leading the group, paused for a moment. He didn't speak, but his body tensed, his eyes scanning the horizon.

Quinn was the first to speak, always the one to spot danger, even when it was miles off. "We're being followed," she muttered, her voice low.

Kane didn't reply immediately. Instead, he reached for the weapons belt he wore across his chest, his fingers brushing against the cold steel of his prized firearms. I could see the hesitation in his eyes, the battle within him. For all his talk of survival and pragmatism, those weapons were more than just tools for him—they were a symbol of who he had been, of the man he had chosen to be before he met us.

But the engines grew louder, closer. The rumble of motorcycles echoed off the barren landscape, and the group's mood shifted from quiet tension to something darker. It was clear: they meant to rob us, or worse.

Kane didn't hesitate any longer. With a sharp exhale, he unhooked one of his guns—his favourite—and handed it to me. "Take it," he said, his voice almost emotionless. "You'll need it."

I stared at the weapon, confused. "What about you?"

His gaze flicked to the others—Zara, Quinn, and me. His face was unreadable, but I could see the change in him. There was a vulnerability there now, one that wasn't part of the man he used to be. "I'll hold them off," he said, turning away before I could argue.

Before I could say anything, he was off, disappearing into the shadows of the wreckage-strewn landscape. The sound of his boots faded as the rest of us huddled behind what little cover we could find.

The ambush came fast. At first, it was just a blur of movement—motorcycles skidding to a halt, figures jumping out of vehicles, weapons drawn. They were no amateurs. They knew what they were doing. But as they closed in on us, something unexpected happened. Kane didn't shoot. Instead, he threw himself into the fray, not with his usual cold, calculating precision, but with raw, unfiltered desperation. He used his body as a shield, pushing us to safety, even as the marauders closed in.

I watched as one of the gang members lunged toward him, and without hesitation, Kane dropped the gun he had just given me and grabbed the man by the throat, knocking him off balance before sending him crashing to the ground. But his actions came at a price. He didn't reach for his weapons. He used his body, his fists, his own strength, and with every blow, I saw the old Kane—ruthless, unyielding, and desperate to protect.

In the end, the fight was won, but not without cost. Kane was breathing hard, sweat dripping from his brow, his eyes wild as he surveyed the wreckage. The weapons he dropped, tools he had relied on for so long, were nowhere to be seen. He had sacrificed them to keep us safe.

It hit me then. He wasn't just protecting us with his actions—he was protecting something inside himself. Maybe he was trying to find a way out of the man he'd been, to change in ways he didn't fully understand yet.

Zara stepped forward, her voice low but full of respect. "You did good," she said, her words surprising me. Kane, always the stoic, the hardened mercenary, didn't flinch. But there was something in his eyes—a flicker of something he didn't want to acknowledge.

As we gathered what we could and moved on, the group was quieter than usual. I couldn't help but wonder if Kane had just taken a step toward something bigger than survival. Something more human.

He had sacrificed more than just some of his weapons that day. He had sacrificed a part of himself. And maybe, just maybe, it was the part that had been holding him back from becoming the person we all needed him to be.

The night had fallen like a heavy cloak, the air thick with the kind of tension that you could almost taste. We were holed up in an old, abandoned farmhouse that had seen better days, the windows boarded up and the doors barricaded with whatever we could find. We hadn't seen the marauders since the ambush, but we all knew they weren't far behind. Kane had taken his usual spot, perched by the window, keeping watch. Zara, in her own way, was keeping herself busy, checking her gear, making sure her sidearm was loaded. Quinn, though, was silent, pacing in the corner like a caged animal, her mind clearly racing.

I could see the fear in her eyes, the hesitation. She'd always been the first to run when things got tough. Every time we'd faced danger, she'd hidden behind Kane or me, never really stepping up. But tonight, it felt different.

The wind howled outside, and I felt a chill run through me—not from the cold, but from the weight of the silence. Kane's hand twitched near his gun, his eyes narrowed as he scanned the horizon. I knew he was trying to stay calm, trying to reassure the group, but even he could sense the danger coming.

Then, we heard it—the faint hum of engines in the distance. It wasn't just one vehicle; it was a whole convoy. My heart skipped a beat. The marauders were coming, and they weren't alone. I could see Kane tense up, his fingers wrapping around his weapon, ready to face whatever came through that door.

But then, something unexpected happened. Quinn, who had been pacing nervously, stopped. I saw her breathe in deeply, her shoulders straightening. For a split second, she looked like a different person—someone determined, someone who wasn't going to run. Her eyes met mine, and there was a flicker of something in them. Something that said she was ready.

"I'm not going anywhere," she said, her voice steady, though I could tell she was holding her breath. "I'm not leaving you guys to do this alone."

It was a small thing, really, just a few words, but it felt like a monumental shift. Quinn had never been the type to face danger head-on. She had always been the first to duck out, the first to hide. But now? She was taking a stand. She was standing with us, and for the first time, I believed she meant it.

Kane looked at her, his expression unreadable, but there was a hint of approval in his eyes. He nodded once, a subtle acknowledgement of her newfound resolve. "Stay close," he said, his voice low but firm. "We'll need everyone for this."

The convoy was getting closer. I could feel the ground rumble underfoot as they neared the farmhouse, the engines roaring louder with each passing second. Quinn's eyes flickered to the door, but she didn't move. Instead, she adjusted her makeshift armour, grabbed a piece of scrap metal that we'd been using to barricade the windows, and stood her ground.

The marauders hit the farmhouse hard, as we knew they would. There was a loud crash as they tried to break through the front door. We all tensed, but instead of retreating, Quinn grabbed her knife and moved to the door with the same determination she had shown moments before. My heart raced as I realized she was preparing to face them head-on.

And she did.

When the door finally buckled under the weight of their attack, Quinn didn't hesitate. She lunged, using the knife with a precision I hadn't known she was capable of. The marauder who'd broken through the door never had a chance. He stumbled back, his eyes wide with shock as Quinn drove the blade home, and for the first time since I'd met her, I saw Quinn not as the scared scavenger, but as someone who could fight—someone who could stand her ground when it mattered most.

The rest of the group moved in quickly, but Quinn was the one who had set the tone. She had faced her fear and taken control of the situation, and in that moment, she had earned our trust. There was no more running for her. She was one of us now, not just by circumstance, but by choice.

As the last of the marauders fled into the night, Kane gave Quinn a silent nod. Zara, who had been watching from the corner, offered a quiet, grudging approval. And I, well, I felt a warmth spread through me—a relief, a pride—for the first time, we were truly a team, and Quinn was part of that team in every sense of the word.

It was a moment that changed everything for us, and for Quinn. We all knew that whatever happened next, we could count on each other. Because when it mattered, Quinn had chosen to stand, and that made all the difference.

The next morning, we were packing up, getting ready to move again. The weight of the past few days had taken its toll. We'd lost supplies in that last skirmish, and the strain was starting to show on all of us. Kane was, as usual, calm and focused, his gaze always scanning for danger. Quinn, after her unexpected bravery, seemed quieter, more introspective, but still alert. Then there was Zara.

I could see it in her eyes. The way she hesitated, looking at her scattered gear, then back at us, clearly trying to justify her actions. Zara had always been about appearances, always worried about how she looked, how she came across. It had cost us before, when she'd been more concerned about saving her personal items than getting us to safety. And now, as we were about to head out, it happened again. In her scramble to grab her weapons, her carefully curated stash of supplies had been left behind—things we could have used, things that could make the difference in getting us through the next few days.

At first, she didn't seem to notice. She was busy straightening her armour, checking her gun like it was the only thing that mattered. I watched her, waiting. I didn't want to say anything. I didn't have to. She knew.

Kane was the first to speak up, his tone calm, but firm. "Zara, we're down supplies. You left the medical kit. The water filters. You need to check yourself before we head out."

Zara froze, her face flushing as she quickly glanced over the pile of scattered supplies. "I—I didn't realize," she stammered, her usual confidence slipping. "I—I thought everything was accounted for."

It was clear she was embarrassed, but it wasn't just the mistake. It was the realization that once again, she had put herself above the group. She had been too focused on what she needed, what she wanted, to think about the bigger picture. I could see the frustration in Kane's eyes, but there was no anger, just a quiet disappointment. He didn't have to say it—he knew, and we all knew.

Quinn, who'd been sitting nearby, looked at Zara and then at me, a mix of concern and understanding on her face. I didn't say anything. I just watched Zara, waiting.

The silence hung in the air for a few moments before Zara spoke again, her voice smaller than usual. "I'm sorry," she said, her gaze dropping to the ground. "I've been... I've been so focused on keeping myself safe that I haven't been thinking about all of you. I'll do better. I'll carry my weight."

It wasn't much, but it was enough. Zara, the woman who had once valued her vanity over everything else, had finally acknowledged her mistake. For the first time, I saw a crack in that hard exterior of hers. She wasn't just a former CorpSec officer trying to protect herself. She was part of the group, and she knew it.

As we packed up the remaining supplies, Zara quietly took charge of organizing the gear, making sure everyone had what they needed. She made sure I had extra water, even though she had barely enough for herself. She double-checked the weapons, the food, the meds. For once, she wasn't just looking after herself. She was looking out for us all, making sure we were ready for whatever came next.

I could see the change in her. It wasn't immediate, and it wasn't perfect, but it was a start. Zara had learned humility the hard way, and for the first time, I felt like we were truly working as a team—everyone contributing, everyone playing their part.

It was a small shift, but it was a powerful one. And in this world, those small shifts were what kept us alive.

The endless stretch of barren land behind us and the distant outline of the border looming ahead like a cruel reminder of how far we'd come. As we drew closer to the heavily militarized U.S.-Canada border, the air seemed to grow colder, the tension thick enough to cut with a knife. The closer we got, the more the landscape changed. It wasn't just the trees that looked more sparse or the sky that seemed darker—it was the soldiers. Their presence was everywhere.

I knew this border had always been heavily guarded, but now it felt more like a fortress. Sentinel CorpSec had taken full control of the area, and remnants of the federal government's forces were still hanging on, trying to maintain some semblance of order. But what order was left? The world we had once known was now a memory, a distant ghost.

As we approached the first checkpoint, the smell of diesel from armored vehicles and the sharp crack of military chatter filled the air. The towering gates, reinforced with metal and concrete, stood like a barrier between us and whatever hope we'd been clinging to. It was strange—this was supposed to be our escape, the place where we could find safety, where we could breathe again. Instead, it felt like the end of the line, a place where all our fears could come crashing down.

Kane led the way, his face set in that usual stoic expression of his, but I could see the weariness behind his eyes. He'd been through enough in his lifetime to know that this wasn't going to be an easy crossing. Zara was still quiet, her hands clenched tightly around her rifle, her eyes scanning the perimeter like a hawk. Quinn, too, was uneasy, her usual bravado gone, replaced by a palpable sense of dread.

We reached the first checkpoint, where two CorpSec officers, dressed in full tactical gear, were checking vehicles and people passing through. They looked like they had all the power in the world, but there was something else there too—a desperation, a thin veneer of control barely masking the chaos below.

Kane didn't hesitate. He knew the game. He knew what it took to get past. Without a word, he walked toward the officers, head held high, his body language projecting authority and confidence. But as we got closer, I could feel the tension in the air. It wasn't just us. It was everyone. The people crossing, the soldiers, the looming sense of danger that seemed to pulse through every inch of the ground beneath our feet.

The officers didn't look happy to see us. Of course, they wouldn't—travellers like us were a rare sight here, and not the kind of people they wanted crossing. They were all too familiar with the stories—the ones about desperate refugees, insurgents, and the rest of the broken world trying to make its way into Canada.

"Where you heading?" one of them barked, his eyes narrowing as he sized us up.

"Just passing through," Kane replied smoothly, his tone neutral but firm. "We've got family in Canada."

The officer didn't seem convinced. He eyed the group, scrutinizing each of us, as if trying to detect some hidden threat in our eyes. When his gaze landed on Zara, I saw a flicker of recognition, something darker behind the surface. He didn't say anything, but it was clear he'd identified her as former CorpSec.

"I'll need to see your papers," the officer said, his voice sharp.

Kane didn't flinch. He handed over a set of forged documents, the kind he'd probably used more times than he cared to count. The officer took them, running them through a scanner with a look of suspicion. It felt like an eternity before the machine beeped, indicating the papers were clean. Still, the officer didn't look happy.

"Keep moving," he grumbled, waving us through with a scowl. "But don't make any noise. You're not welcome here."

We walked past, my heart racing in my chest, and I could feel Quinn's breath quickening beside me. It wasn't over yet. This was only the first checkpoint, and we had a long way to go before we could even think about crossing into Canada. Every step felt heavier than the last, as if the weight of the world had suddenly settled on our shoulders.

But as we moved forward, I saw something shift in Kane. It wasn't much, just the faintest loosening of his posture, the slightest easing of his tension. He wasn't letting his guard down—not even close—but for the first time in a long while, he seemed to be letting himself believe that maybe, just maybe, we were going to make it.

I wasn't so sure, but I couldn't help but hope, too.

The wind was biting, carrying with it the distant hum of engines and the sharp crackle of radios. We had made it past the first checkpoint, but I could feel the danger closing in. I wasn't sure how long we'd be able to keep up the ruse. Sentinel CorpSec was everywhere—hidden in plain sight, watching every move we made. It was just a matter of time before someone figured out our papers were fake.

We were nearing the second checkpoint when it happened. Kane's eyes flicked to the right, his face hardening, and without a word, he pulled us off the path, ducking behind a cluster of rusted vehicles. My heart skipped a beat as the sound of heavy boots echoed in the distance, followed by a shout.

"Hey! You—stop!"

The realization hit me like a ton of bricks. They'd found out. Someone had checked our papers. The game was over.

Kane grabbed Zara and Quinn, pulling them down into the dirt with him. I could hear the shouts now, the crackle of weapons being drawn. I squeezed my rifle tighter, my hands trembling, but Kane's steady presence was like a rock beside me. He turned to us, his voice low, urgent.

"Stay close. Keep quiet. We move on my mark."

We huddled together, barely breathing, while the CorpSec soldiers fanned out, their shadows stretching long in the dim light. The tension was suffocating. I could hear my own heartbeat, pounding in my ears. I wasn't sure how we were going to get out of this. Not like this. Not now.

But then, with a sudden, terrifying clarity, I saw the first soldier coming around the corner of a building—rifle raised, scanning the area. He was too close. We had no time. No time at all.

"Move!" Kane shouted.

Without thinking, we darted to our feet, and in that split second, all hell broke loose. The first shot rang out, followed by the deafening crack of gunfire. We were already running, zigzagging for cover as the soldiers opened fire, their bullets tearing through the air around us.

I glanced back—just for a second—and saw one of the soldiers take aim at Kane. My stomach dropped. I didn't have time to process it. I couldn't. I just moved, running as fast as I could, weaving between the abandoned vehicles and piles of debris.

Then, I heard the scream.

Quinn.

I whipped around, my breath catching in my throat. Quinn had fallen behind, her leg caught by one of the bullets, blood seeping quickly from the wound. She was clutching her leg, her face pale with pain, but she was trying to crawl, trying to get back to us.

I hesitated. For a split second, the world around me slowed. I was about to run back to her when Kane grabbed my arm, pulling me forward.

"Not now! We have to keep moving!"

But I could see it in his eyes—the conflict, the moment of hesitation. For a second, I thought he might break from his usual stoic nature and go back for Quinn. But he didn't. We kept running, our footsteps pounding in the dirt as the sounds of gunfire echoed behind us.

We had made it a few hundred yards when I glanced over my shoulder again. Quinn was still struggling, but she wasn't going to make it on her own. A few more steps, and I could see the CorpSec soldiers closing in, almost on top of her.

The decision was made for me.

I broke from the group, ignoring Kane's frantic shouts, and sprinted back toward Quinn. Every step felt like an eternity. The pain in my chest from the fear was suffocating, but I couldn't leave her behind. I couldn't.

I reached her just as one of the soldiers was about to take another shot. I didn't think, just acted. I tackled him to the ground, my weight knocking him off balance. The gun went skittering across the dirt, and I could hear Quinn's laboured breathing behind me. She was still alive, but barely.

Kane was right behind me now, moving like a shadow, pulling the soldier off me and throwing him aside with a practised ease. He didn't even flinch as he grabbed Quinn, hoisting her onto his back without a second thought.

"Move!" Kane barked, his voice low but filled with urgency.

We didn't have much time. I could hear the others still coming. But I could also hear Quinn's weak voice, her words barely audible, but the pain in them unmistakable.

"I—I'm sorry... I can't..."

"You're not dying today," I said, my voice steady despite the storm of fear raging inside me.

With one final look over my shoulder, I turned and followed Kane, pushing myself harder than I ever thought I could. We moved through the wreckage, our breaths coming in short, sharp bursts as the sounds of battle faded into the background. But the weight of it all lingered—the loss, the sacrifice.

We had made it through, but at what cost?

The group was broken, but we were still alive. That was something, at least. It had to be enough.

The sight of the asylum centre was almost too much to believe. After everything we had been through—escaping gunfire, the uncertainty, the constant fear—we were finally here. Canada. We had made it.

The building loomed in front of us, its tall, iron gates standing open as a steady stream of people shuffled in and out. It wasn't much to look at—cracked windows, worn-down walls—but to me, it felt like the gates of heaven. I could hear my breath, deep and uneven, but I didn't care. I could almost taste the relief in the air.

We moved toward the entrance, every step feeling lighter than the last. Kane was still carrying Quinn, but his pace had slowed, the weight of her injury starting to drag him down. Despite his tough exterior, I could tell he was struggling. Zara walked beside me, her eyes scanning the horizon, always alert, but there was something different in her stride. She seemed... softer. Less consumed by herself. Quinn, on the other hand, was drifting in and out of consciousness, her face pale but alive, and that was all that mattered.

At the gates, a pair of guards stood, looking us over with practised eyes. One of them, a woman with sharp features and a deep frown, stepped forward as we approached.

"Are you the ones from the border?" she asked, her voice steady but guarded.

I nodded, my throat dry. "We are."

She studied us for a moment, her gaze lingering on Quinn, who was still slumped over Kane's back, breathing raggedly.

"You're lucky you made it this far," the guard said, stepping aside. "Come on in. We'll get you settled."

As we crossed the threshold into the centre, I felt a wave of exhaustion crash over me. The pressure that had been building in my chest for so long seemed to dissipate, though it didn't vanish entirely. There was still so much I didn't understand, so many pieces of the puzzle left to fit together. But for now, I had to focus on the present.

We were safe. At least for the moment.

The inside of the asylum centre was bustling with activity. People hurried past us—families with small children, individuals wrapped in heavy coats, their faces weary but hopeful. We were directed to a small medical area where Quinn was taken immediately for treatment. Zara went off to speak with someone in charge about the group's status, leaving me standing there, alone with Kane.

We didn't speak for a while. He had set Quinn down on a cot, and he was standing by, watching as the doctors moved around her, working quickly to stabilize her. He looked different, like a man who had finally let go of something heavy. The walls he had built around himself had crumbled a little, and though the change was subtle, it was there.

Eventually, Kane turned to me, his voice softer than I had ever heard it. "You did good back there," he said. "We all did."

I nodded, the words not quite reaching my lips. We had done good, but we had also lost. There was a hole in our group now. Quinn would recover, but things would never be the same.

"I don't know what's next," I said quietly. "But for now... we're safe. And that has to count for something."

Kane looked at me for a long moment before glancing away. "Yeah. It does."

As we sat there, waiting for the doctors to finish with Quinn and the others to return, the weight of everything that had happened—the people we'd lost, the dangers we'd faced—finally began to settle in. But for the first time in a long while, I felt a glimmer of hope.

We had made it. And somehow, that was enough for now.

Sitting quietly in the sterile waiting room of the asylum centre, I couldn't help but reflect on everything that had led me here. My fingers absently traced the edge of a worn-out bench as my mind wandered back to the days before the coma—the life I had once known, the people I thought I understood. So much had changed, and yet, here I was, in a place that felt both unfamiliar and strangely comforting. Safe, for now, but changed, in ways I couldn't entirely grasp.

When I first woke up in that hospital, I had no idea what year it was or how the world had crumbled. The hospital had seemed like a dream, too quiet, too removed from everything I knew. But the truth had hit me in pieces—shattered by each new revelation, each new step I took out into that dystopian world. I had barely known what I was doing, stumbling from one frightening encounter to the next, unsure of how to survive, let alone how to trust.

But then came Kane. Quiet, stoic, hard as stone, but with a vulnerability hidden deep beneath. I had watched him, even when he didn't know it, wrestle with himself. At first, he seemed like the last person who would care about anyone other than himself. But I had seen the shift, the way he'd started to open up—not to me, necessarily, but to something bigger, something worth fighting for. The Kane I had met in the beginning was gone, replaced by someone who had come to care about more than just surviving. That shift—his growth—had been a quiet revolution, one that had affected all of us.

And then there was Quinn. Scared, running from danger, always the first to think of escape. But I saw something change in her too, slowly at first, almost imperceptible. She had started to stand her ground, to fight back, to care about the people around her, even when it scared her. It wasn't easy for her, but I could see it now, how she'd taken a step out of her own shadow. She had grown. And I had grown with her.

Zara. Oh, Zara. I used to think she was nothing but vanity wrapped in a CorpSec badge. She had seemed so sure of herself, like she had everything figured out, everything under control. But I had learned that she, too, had her battles. Her past, her fears, her reasons for wanting to get to Canada—they weren't as simple as I had once thought. We had learned to rely on each other, and in doing so, I saw Zara begin to change. She didn't let her pride rule her anymore. She started to understand that survival wasn't about standing alone. It was about standing together.

The truth was, I didn't know who I was when I first woke up. I had no idea what had happened to the world, to my family, to the life I once took for granted. But somewhere along the way, I had learned something invaluable. The world hadn't just broken around us; we had broken, too. But we didn't have to stay broken. We had the power to rebuild, to change, to grow, if we just kept moving forward.

As I sat there, staring at the sterile white walls, I realized how much I had changed. I wasn't the person who had woken up in that hospital. I was someone else now—stronger, braver, more aware of the world and the people in it. The journey had been hard, and it wasn't over, not by a long shot. But I knew one thing for certain: I wasn't alone. I had my companions, and together, we had found something worth fighting for. Something worth living for.

The doors to the medical room opened, and I stood, brushing off the thoughts that had started to drift away. Kane and Quinn had been through so much, and there was still so much to face, but for the first time in a long time, I felt like maybe we could face it. Together.

As I sat in the sterile waiting room of the asylum centre, my thoughts wandered again, this time to the stark contrast between Canada and the country we had just fled. America, once a beacon of democracy and opportunity, had turned into a nightmare—a world ruled by corporatocracies, where survival wasn't just about being strong, but about who had the right connections, who controlled the resources, and who could afford to buy their way to safety. In that world, humanity seemed like an afterthought.

But here, in Canada, things felt different. The lines weren't as blurred. Yes, the government had its issues, but there was a sense of order, a sense that the people still mattered. Canada had responded to America's collapse with a sense of compassion that seemed almost foreign to me now. Where America had abandoned its citizens, Canada had opened its arms. While the states burned, Canada made a concerted effort to take in refugees, to offer asylum to those seeking safety, to those whose lives had been destroyed by forces beyond their control.

I couldn't help but marvel at the contrast. America had fallen victim to the same forces that had been gnawing at the world for decades—greed, corruption, and the unchecked power of corporations. But Canada, while not without its own problems, had managed to hold onto something far more precious: a sense of duty to its people, to the displaced, to those who had nowhere else to turn. The very fact that I was sitting here, safe for the moment, was proof of that difference.

The more I thought about it, the more I realized how deep the divide ran. While America had allowed its soul to be devoured by corporate interests, Canada had retained a semblance of humanity. It wasn't perfect—no country ever is—but it was a world away from the nightmare we'd left behind. The Canadian response wasn't just a political move or a strategic one. It was a humanitarian one. A chance for people like me to rebuild, to hope again, when hope had seemed like a distant memory in America.

I couldn't help but feel a wave of gratitude as I thought about it. For all the uncertainty ahead, Canada felt like a place where I could at least begin to heal. Where the rules weren't written by the highest bidder. Where I wasn't just a number on a corporate ledger. Here, I could be human again. And in that moment, the weight of everything we had endured felt a little lighter, knowing that there were places in the world that still saw people—not as products, but as people.

# July 25, The Future

As I sat there, the weight of everything that had happened over the past weeks pressed heavily on me. The journey had been long, painful, and full of uncertainty. My body was exhausted, my mind frayed from the constant tension, but now, in this relative peace, I found myself facing a question I hadn't allowed myself to think about until now: What comes next?

I had been running from a country that had become unrecognizable. America was no longer the land of opportunity, but a broken shell of what it once was. It was a place where the powerful had seized control and used it to keep the rest of the population under their thumb. Where people were forced to live in fear, where women like me were seen as little more than commodities to be controlled. My heart ached for those still trapped in that nightmare, the ones left behind, the ones who didn't have the chance to escape. I couldn't just forget them. I couldn't pretend they weren't still out there, struggling in a world that no longer cared.

But then, there was Canada. This new world, where safety didn't feel like a distant dream. The very idea of starting fresh, of building a life where I could breathe again, was tempting. I could settle here, find work, make a home. I could do what I needed to do to heal from everything I had been through. But the thought of leaving behind those I had known, those who were still suffering, gnawed at me. Would I be doing the right thing? Would I be abandoning my people by walking away?

I could feel the pull in both directions. There was a part of me that longed for peace, for a place where I didn't have to constantly look over my shoulder, where I could find some semblance of normalcy. But there was another part of me that wanted to fight, to go back and help those who couldn't escape. The fight wasn't just about survival anymore. It was about justice. It was about giving a voice to those who had been silenced, those who had been left behind in the ashes of a broken nation.

But could I really go back? Could I face the nightmare again, knowing how much had changed? What kind of difference could I make, just one person in a world of corruption and violence? Could I find others who were willing to stand with me, who weren't afraid to fight for what was right?

I didn't have the answers, not yet. But as I sat in that asylum centre, the possibility of both options felt like an impossible choice. The weight of the world, the weight of so many lost lives, was pressing down on me. My heart told me I couldn't ignore it, that I couldn't let the suffering continue without trying to do something about it. But my mind... my mind knew that there was still so much more I needed to understand about this new world, about the ones I had left behind, before I could make a decision.

So for now, I would rest. I would let myself breathe, let the dust settle. But I knew deep down that this wasn't the end. Whatever came next, it would be a fight. The question was: would I be fighting for those I had left behind or for the future I was beginning to build for myself? That answer wasn't clear yet. But it would come. It had to.

The day had come when we all knew it was time to go our separate ways. It had been a journey like no other, one that had changed us in ways we could hardly understand, let alone explain. What had started as a desperate flight for survival had become something more. We had all found pieces of ourselves along the way—pieces we didn't know were missing until we had the courage to look for them. But now, we were in Canada, safe for the moment, and it felt like the right time for each of us to begin a new chapter.

Kane was the first to speak up. He had always been a man of few words, but now, as we stood together in that final quiet moment, there was a shift in him. The hardened exterior, the ruthless enforcer, had softened, even if just a little. He turned to us, his voice steady but with a hint of something different behind it.

"I've got my own path to follow," he said, his eyes scanning each of us in turn. "This... whatever we were to each other, it's over now. But it's not just about survival anymore. It's about rebuilding. Maybe that means starting somewhere else. Maybe it means doing the right thing for once."

I could tell he was trying to figure out what that looked like for him, but the truth was, I could see the change in him. He didn't have all the answers, but the fact that he was even thinking about doing the right thing meant something. It was a quiet victory, one that didn't need to be shouted from the rooftops.

Quinn, standing a little to the side, had her arms crossed, her gaze somewhere far off. She'd come so far from the scared, uncertain person we had met in Austin. I saw it in her posture, the way she stood taller now, no longer shying away from the world around her. She glanced over at me, a soft smile tugging at the corners of her mouth.

"I guess I'm not running anymore," she said with a wry chuckle. "I never thought I'd end up here, but there's something to be said for facing your fears. I'll figure it out. I think it's time I stop running from life."

She had grown in ways I hadn't expected. Maybe she didn't have all the answers either, but that was okay. The fact that she was ready to stop running meant something. It meant she was willing to take responsibility, to face the world as it was and figure out how to live in it.

Zara, on the other hand, was still the same as ever, a little brash, a little self-centred, but I saw a shift in her too. She wasn't just concerned about herself anymore. She had learned to care, to think beyond her own desires. She stood a little closer to the group now, not so distant.

"I've still got a long way to go," she admitted, looking down at the CorpSec badge in her hand. "But I'm not going back to that life. I'll find something else. Something better. And I'll make sure I don't forget where I came from."

I wasn't sure what the future held for any of us, but for the first time in a long time, I felt a flicker of hope. We had each changed, maybe in ways that couldn't be undone. And while none of us knew exactly what lay ahead, we had found purpose—something that had been missing from all of our lives before this journey began.

As for me, I had come to a quiet decision. I knew I had to keep moving forward, just like the others. I couldn't stop here.

There were too many people still suffering in America, too many who hadn't had the chance to escape, who didn't have the luxury of finding safety in Canada. I couldn't forget them, not after everything we had seen and been through. But for now, I needed to take a step back, to figure out what I could do from here. Could I help them? Could I fight for what was right, for those still trapped in the mess America had become?

One thing was for sure. This wasn't the end of the road for any of us. The journey would continue, each of us carving out our own paths, but forever changed by what we had shared. I couldn't wait to see where those paths would lead.